D0349538

To my two children,
Luke and Hayley
~ *PK*

To Raechele and Jim
~*JC*

This edition produced for
THE BOOK PEOPLE LTD
Hall Wood Avenue, Haydock, St Helens WA11 9UL, by
LITTLE TIGER PRESS
an imprint of Magi Publications
1 The Coda Centre, 189 Munster Road, London SW6 6AW
www.littletigerpress.com

First published in Great Britain 2002

Text © Peter Kavanagh 2002
Illustrations © Jane Chapman 2002
Peter Kavanagh and Jane Chapman have asserted their rights
to be identified as the author and illustrator of this
work under the Copyright, Designs and Patents Act, 1988.
All rights reserved • ISBN 1 85430 806 8

A CIP catalogue record for this book is available from the British Library

Printed in Belgium by Proost NV

PETER KAVANAGH

JANE CHAPMAN

Love
Like
This

TED SMART

The pale sun rises through morning mist.
We go walking together on days like this.

When storm winds blow we
shelter together. Nothing can
harm us while we have each other.

Later we chase across hot dusty plains,
stomping and stamping and playing new games.

When the bright sun rises
hotter and higher, we stride along
by the cool fast river.

The water is clean and we're covered in dust. We jump in together and let it wash over us.

We dip and dive and splash and splish.
Fun like this is all we could wish.

We walk in the grass to dry in the sun
and sing together in trumpeting fun.

Sometimes we laugh for no reason at all,
comparing our trunks, one big, one small.

We gaze at the birds flying into the night
and the stars in the sky, all twinkly and bright.

And when we lie in the soft dewy grass,
you tell me elephant tales from the past.

Last thing at night we curl in a hug,
safe and happy, cosy and snug.

And we sink into sleep and dream of new days.
Love like this is love always.